Marvin
Dresses Up

Written by
Michèle Dufresne

Illustrated by
Ann Caranci

PIONEER VALLEY EDUCATIONAL PRESS, INC.

Look at me.
I am a lion.

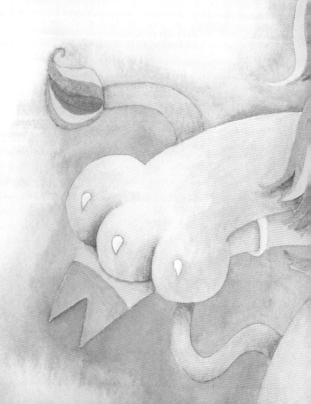

3

Look at me.
I am a rabbit.

5

Look at me.
I am a cat.

6

Look at me.
I am a dog.

9

Look at me.
I am a bird.

11

Look at me.
I am an elephant.

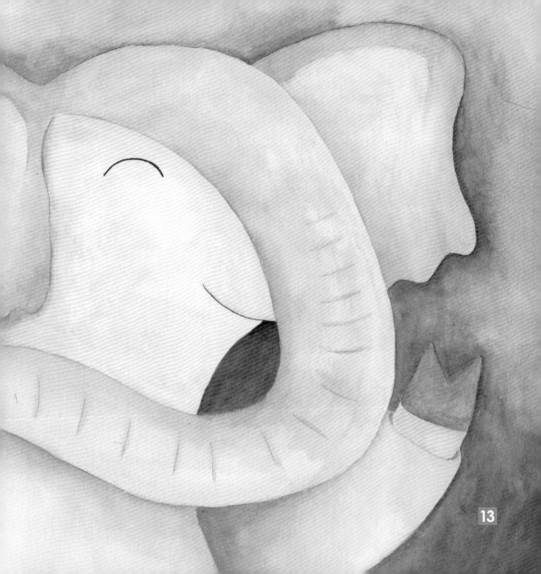

Look at me.
I am a crocodile.

Look at me.
I am a pig!

16

Marvin Pig Set 1

Going Places
Marvin Has Fun
Marvin Dresses Up
Marvin's Friends
Look Out for the Lion
Catching Fireflies

PIONEER VALLEY BOOKS

pioneervalleybooks.com

Marvin Pig Set 1
Marvin Dresses Up
Word Count: 56